To all the kids and the kids at heart.

Print ISBN: 978-1-54395-852-2

eBook ISBN: 978-1-54395-853-9

Sunny's New Wings

by Kevin Wadee

Past the field of honey-colored daffodils, beyond Fairy Falls, and deep within the forest, was Maple Grove. It was where trees always stood tall and the flowers never stopped blooming. Leaves were green even in winter. That was because Maple Grove was no ordinary forest. It was surrounded by magic.

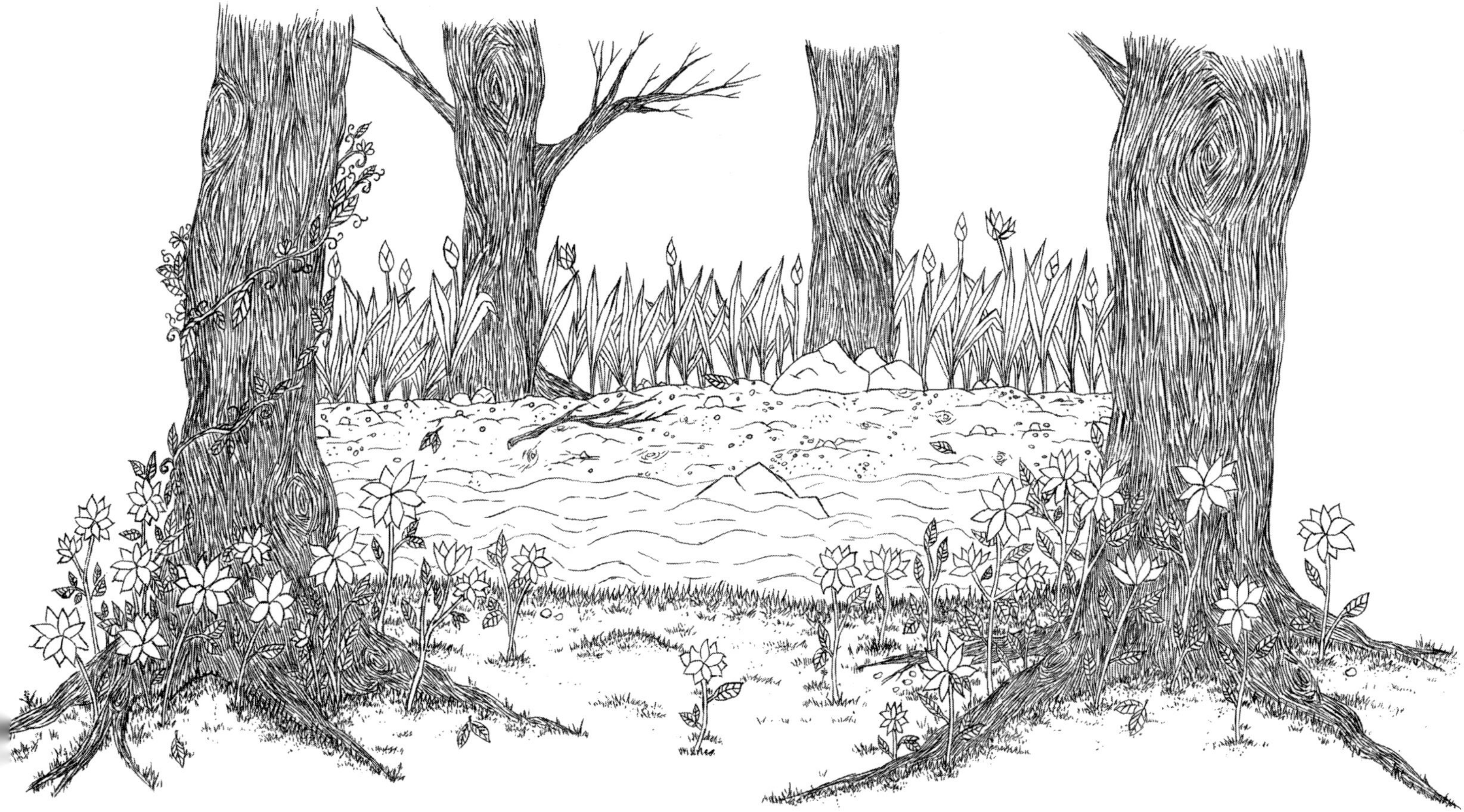

The clearing was a home to elves, fairies and all kinds of magical creatures you can imagine. Some were tall, some were short. Some big and some small. Some were very good and some were very naughty. But they all came together and made Maple Grove a happy home.

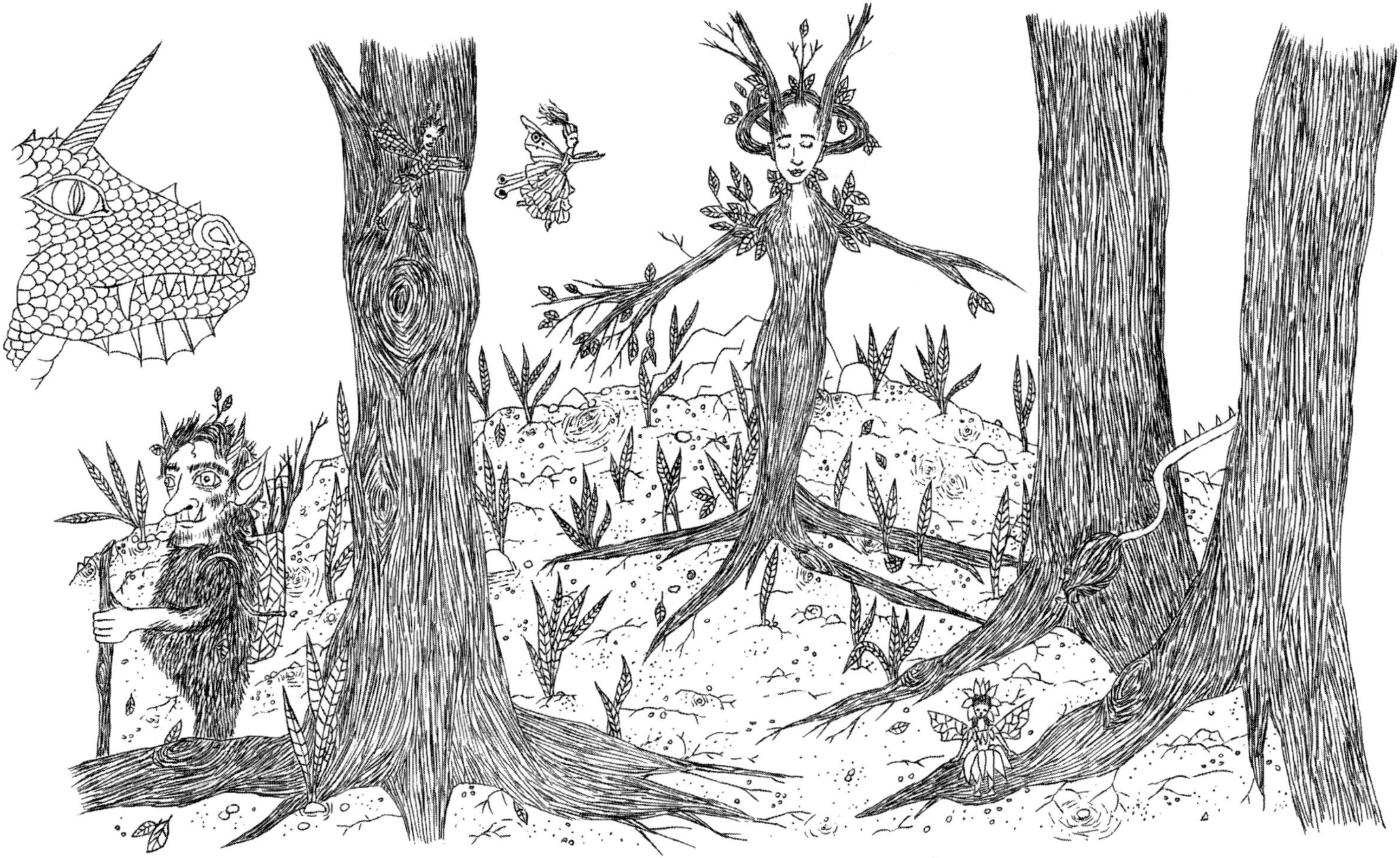

Sunny Seedpod was happily sitting on a rock by the edge of a water spring. The pool of cool water was surrounded by big, red toadstools. His fairy friends loved playing in the water and drinking from it.

Sunny was a good little elf. He would get himself into trouble now and then but he promised his mother that he would always try to be good.

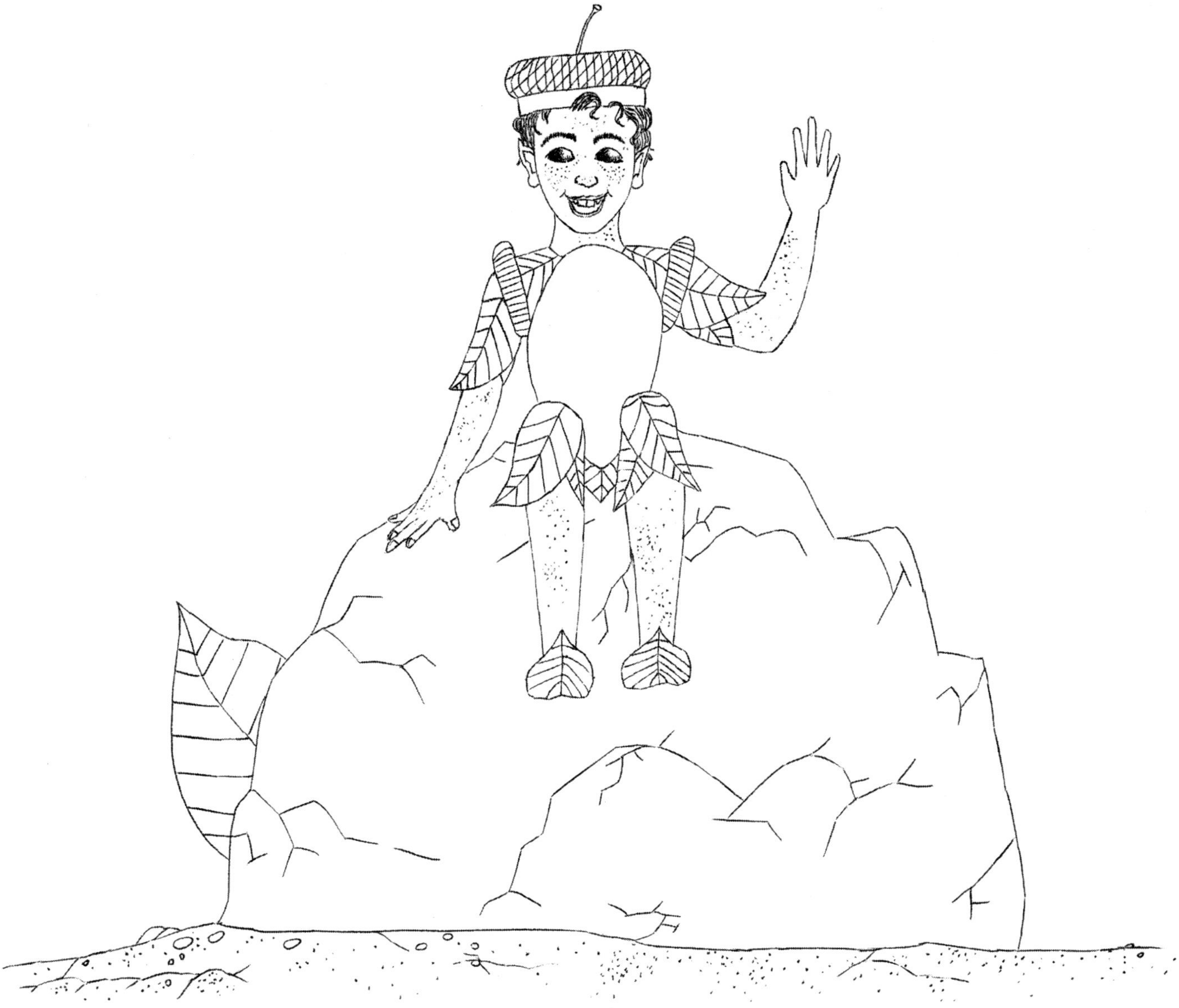

"Come play with us Sunny!" his friends yelled. They were frolicking in the water. Splashing around in the spring did look very fun.

Sunny would love to but he wouldn't want to get his new shoes wet. His mother spent a week weaving them from oak leaves. Long nights by the fire were spent to make sure it perfectly fit his feet. She would be mad if he got them dirty.

So Sunny just smiled and stayed by the edge. Instead, he entertained himself by skipping pebbles by the water.

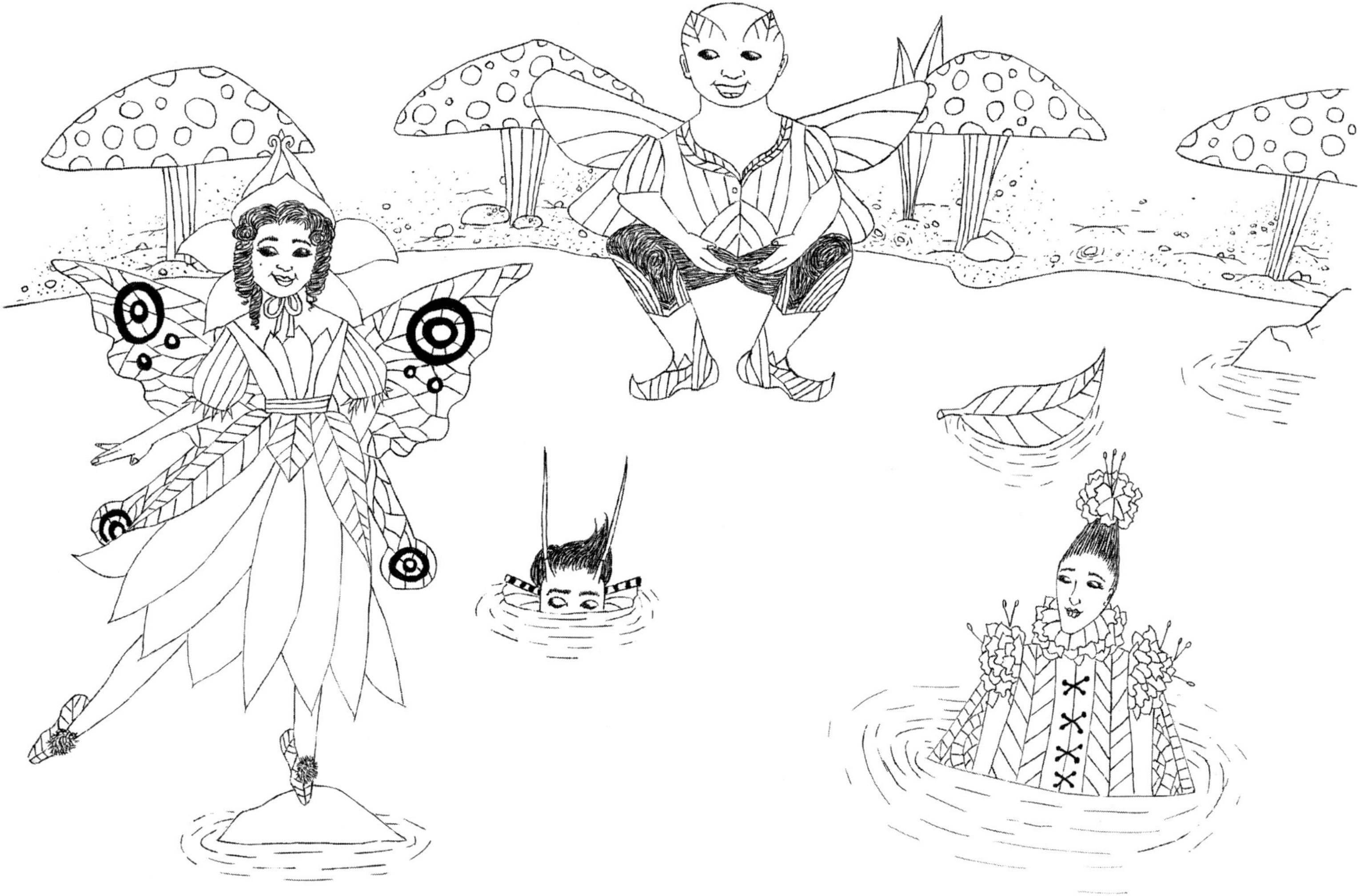

After some time, one of Sunny's fairy friends, Lily, flew towards him. Her beautiful butterfly wings fluttered as she moved. She sat on a toadstool to dry her curly hair. Sunny looked at her wings and sighed. He always wanted wings. He wondered what it was like to be way up in the skies.

The little elf wanted to fly around and do things just like his fairy friends. He hated being left behind. It made him feel terrible. With wings, they could go to places he couldn't reach like the treetops and the mountains. Flying was also much faster. Getting from one spot to another only took seconds. Sunny didn't like how slow his small feet were.

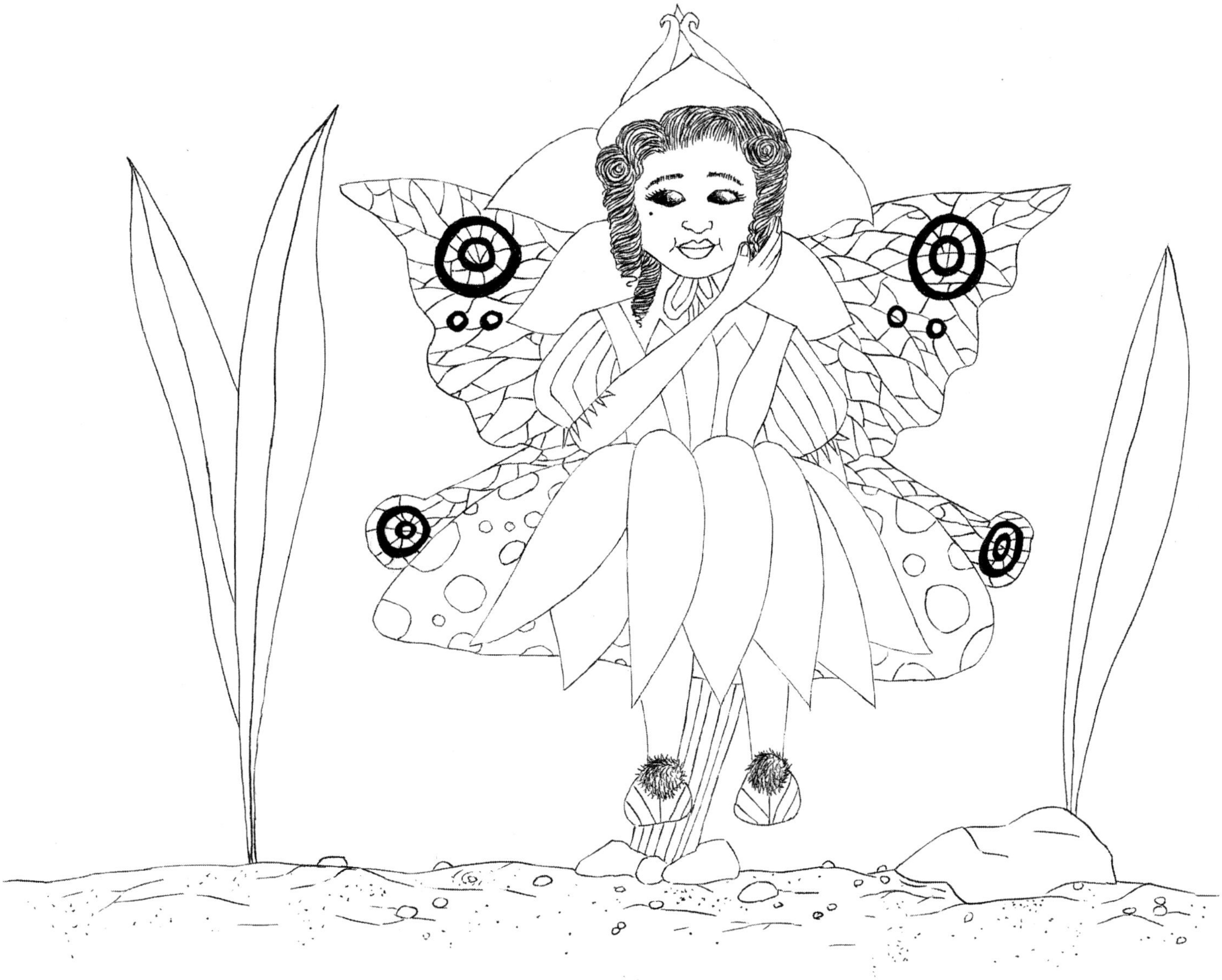

All the fairies dried themselves and went to play among the top branches of the Maple trees. Poor Sunny was left behind again. He had no way of getting to the top of the trees. He couldn't fly like everybody else. With his head down, he sadly walked home.

His mother was waiting for him at home with some warm soup. Sunny and his mother lived inside the hollow of a big oak tree.

"Mama, why don't I have wings?" Sunny asked.

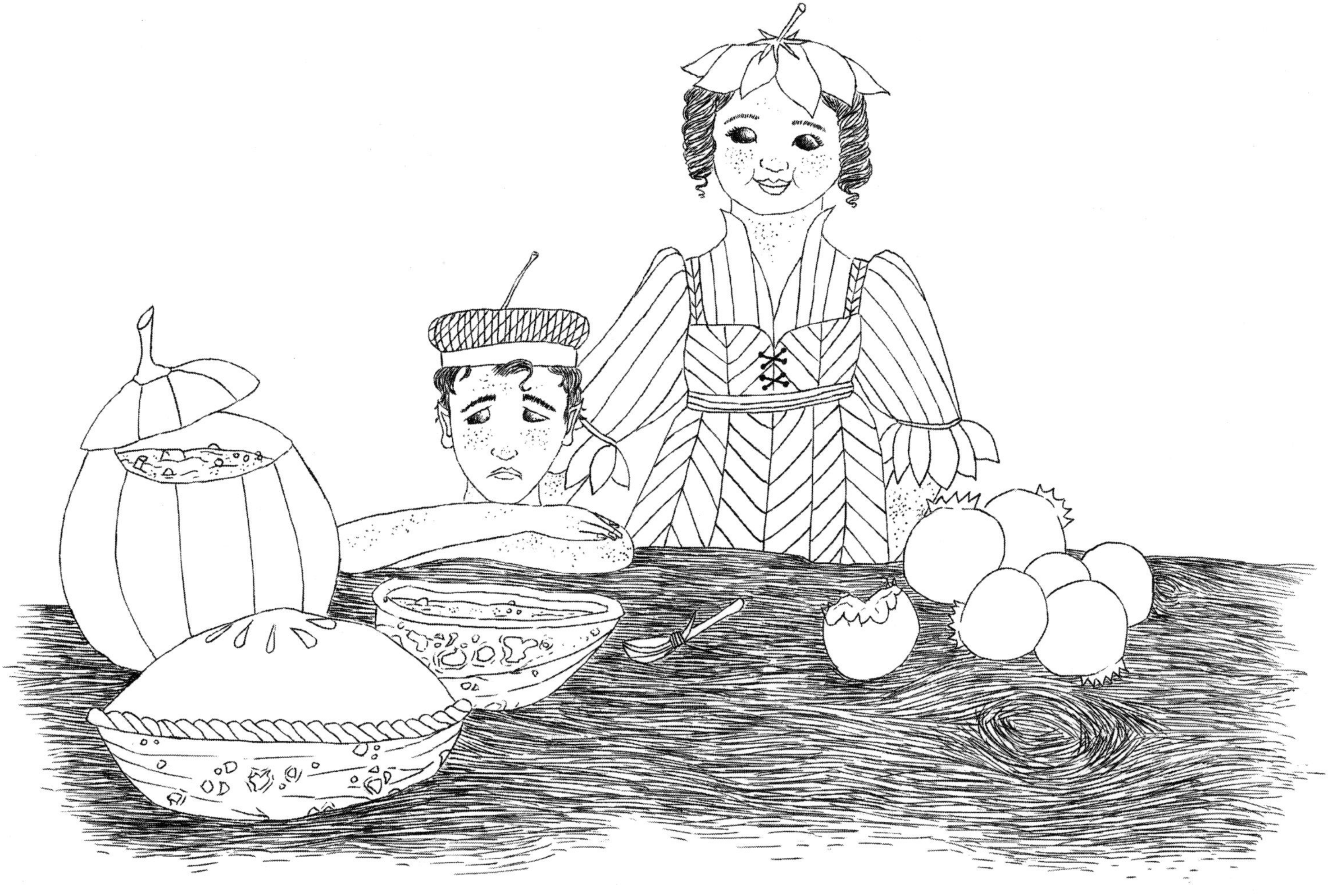

His mother told him that elves don't have wings. He was an elf and he should be proud of it. But Sunny frowned in disappointment. He wondered what he needed to do to have wings of his own. Then, he had an idea. If he didn't have any wings, he was going to make some!

Sunny was going to make his dreams come true.

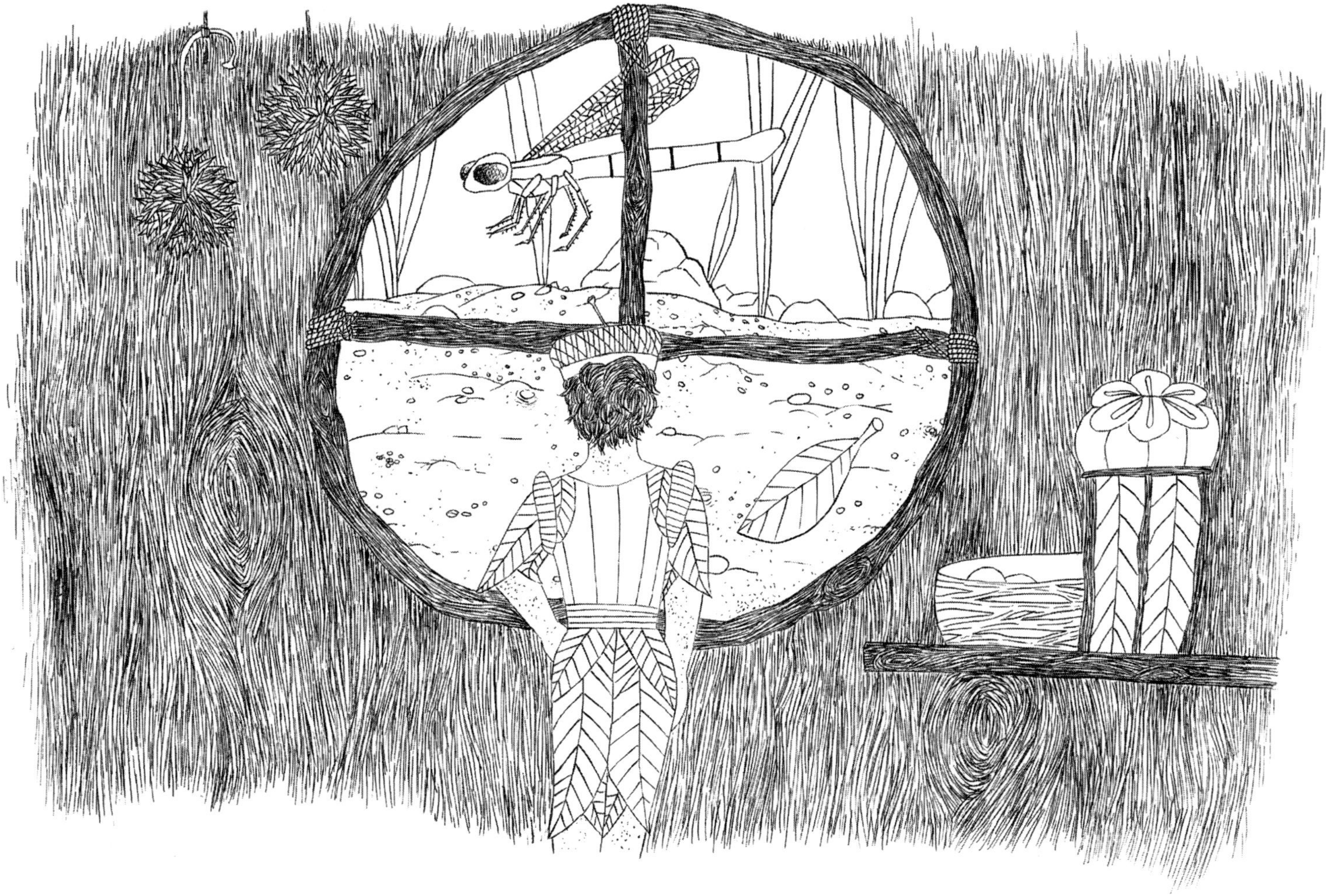

Sunny ran to gather some fallen twigs. He also needed leaves! The day went by quickly. Before he knew, it was already the afternoon.

The little elf needed one last thing on his list. He asked Matilda the Old Spider for some of her sticky spiderweb. When he told her what it was for, she just giggled and said "Don't be silly! There is no such thing as a flying elf!".

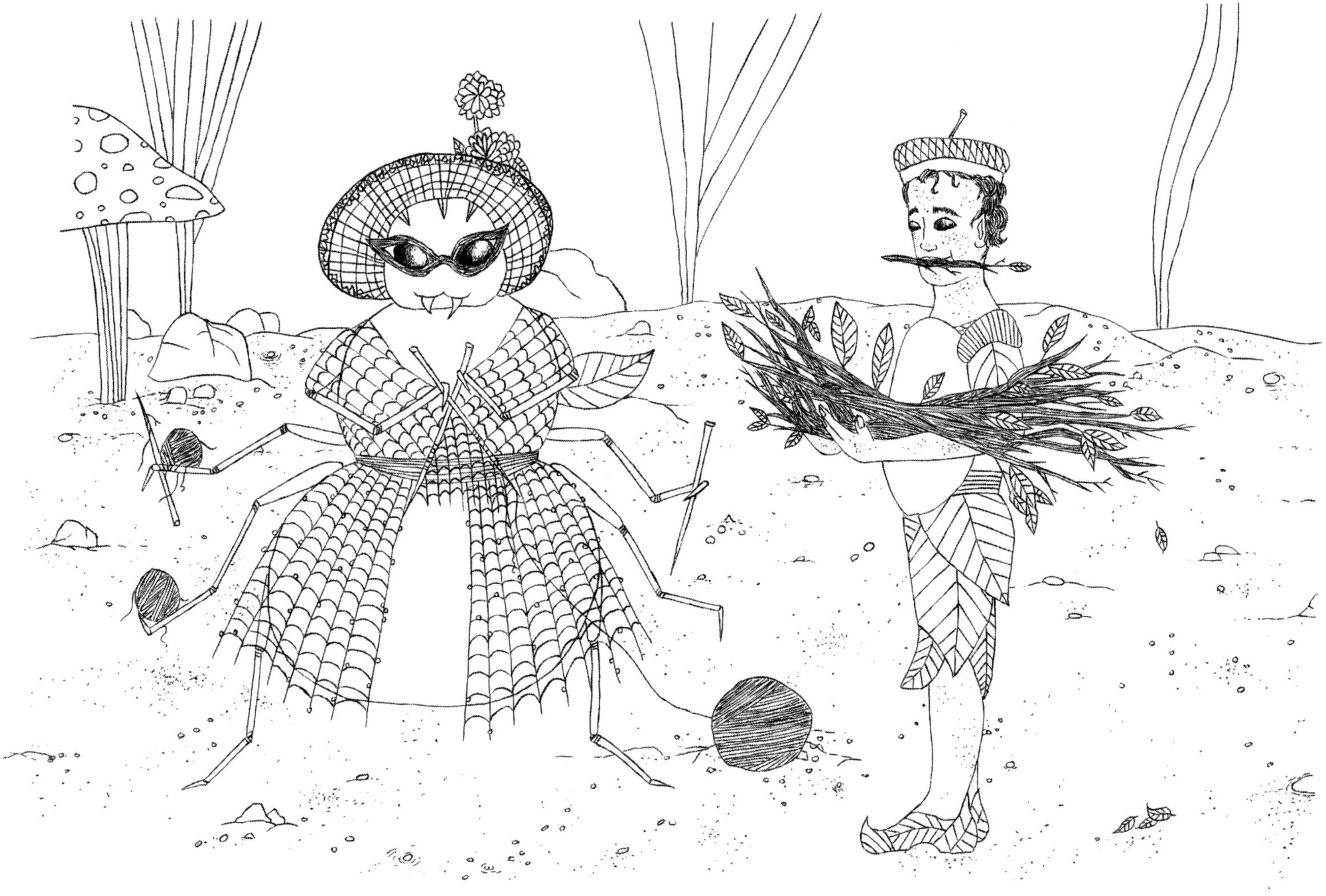

Even when others laughed at him, Sunny was not going
to give up. He wanted wings more than anything.

He thanked her for the web and hurried to build his wings. Following
closely at how a dragonfly's wings worked, Sunny made the frame
of his wings from the twigs. Then, he used thick leaves that wouldn't
fly away from strong winds. After sewing his wings with strings
of spiderweb, he was finally done. It was time to test it out.

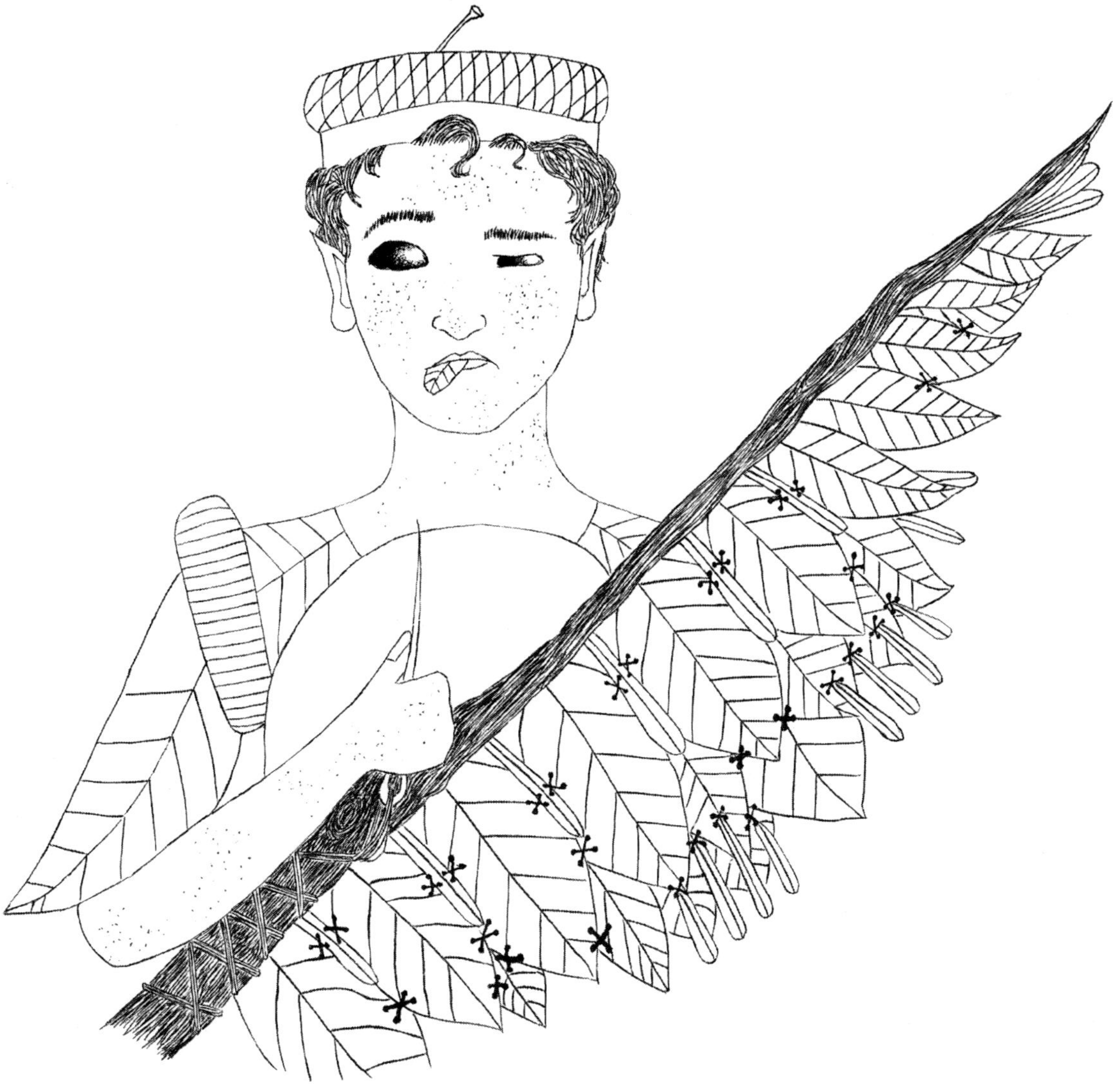

Standing at the edge of a cliff, Sunny took a deep breath.

1...2...3!

Sunny jumped.

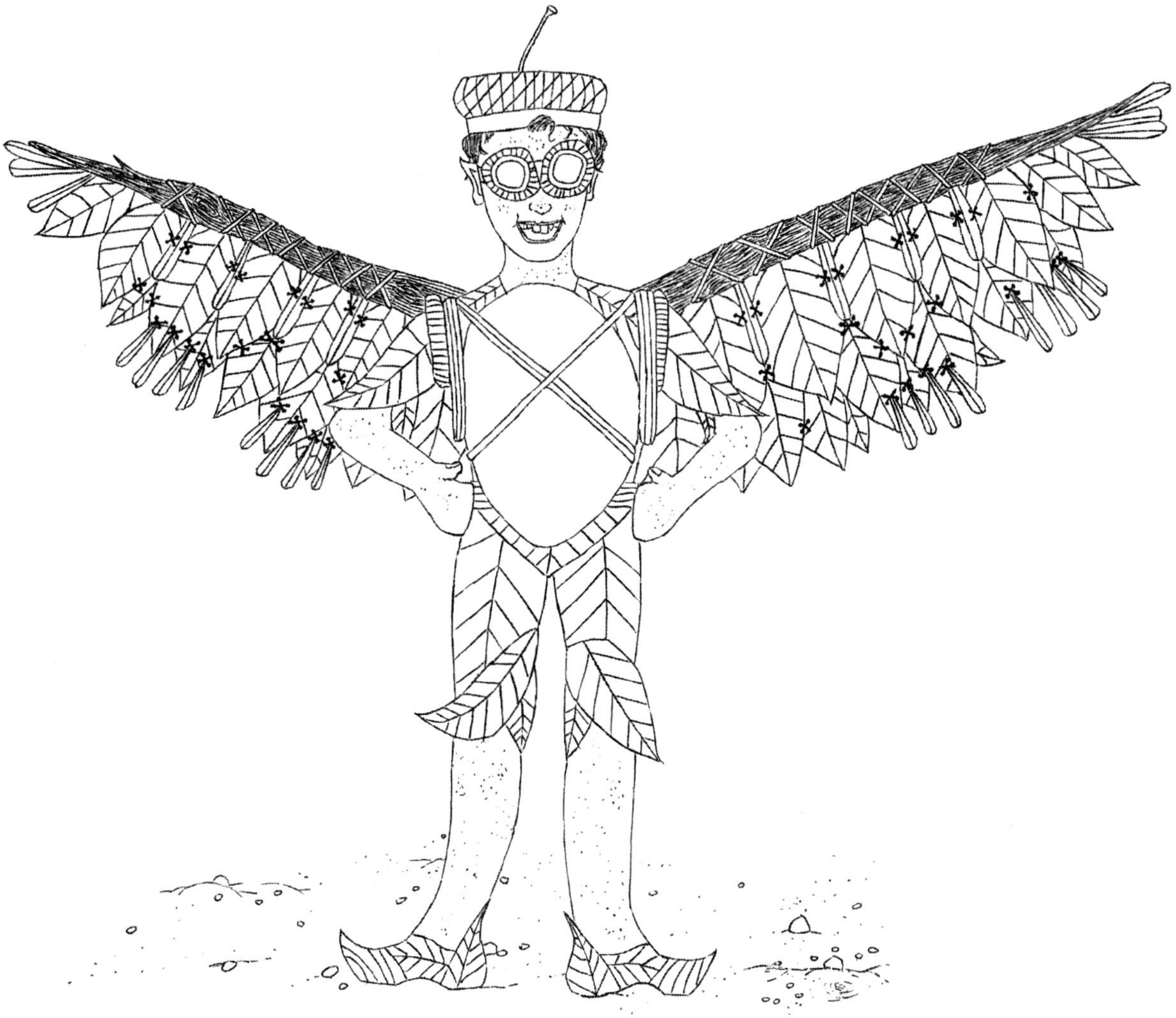

CRASH! The elf was stuck in the bush below! The spiderweb he used to tie the wings together weren't strong enough to hold it in place. It fell apart too quickly in the air.

Sunny frowned. He got out from the bush and dragged his wings back to his house. After some thinking, he smiled once more because now he had another idea!

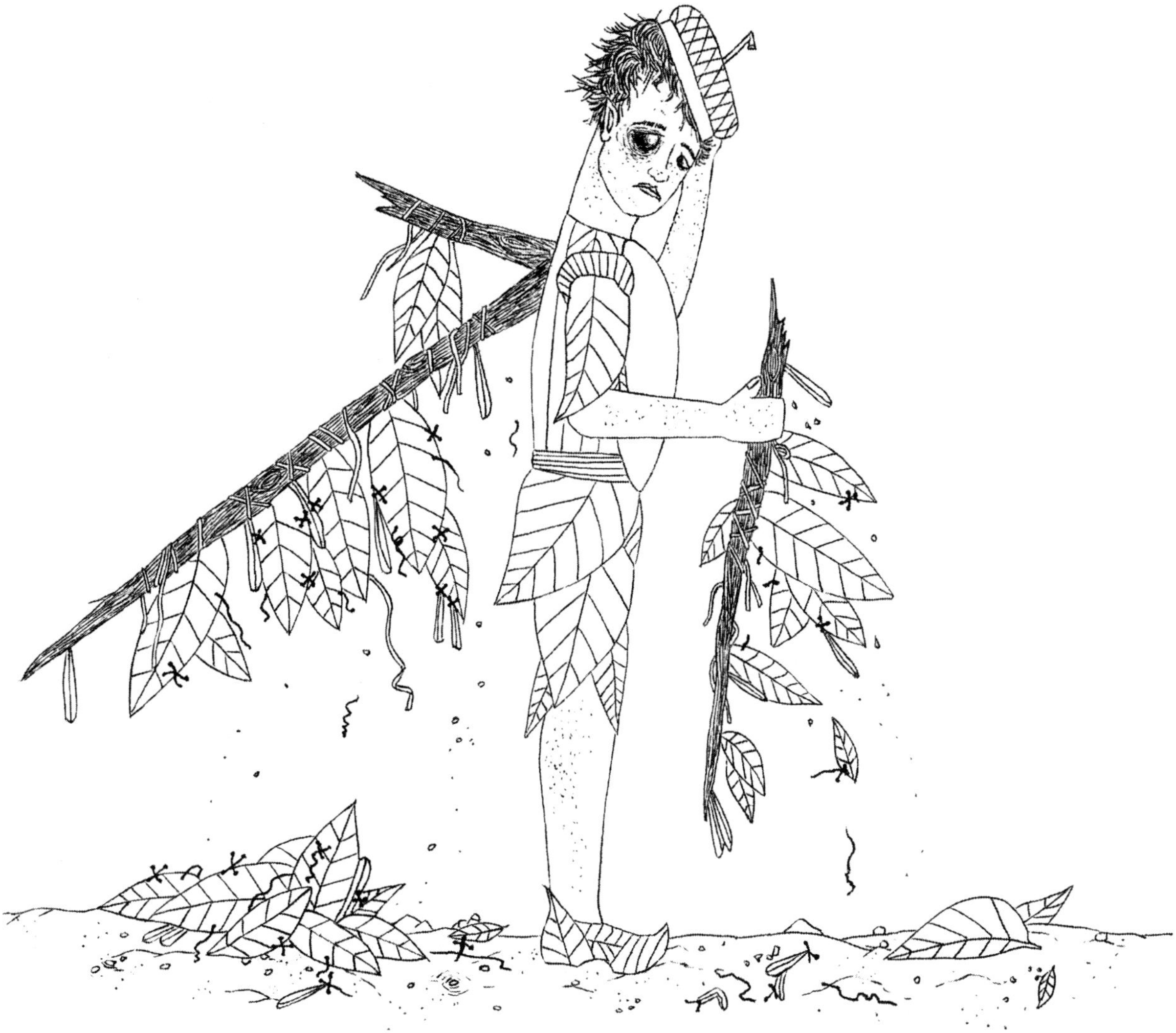

Knock! Knock! Knock! Sunny was knocking on the door of the hive of the Queen Bee. He needed her help. She was sitting on her throne singing a sweet song while her buzzing bees were hard at work. They were collecting pots of honey. Bees do love honey! The Queen touched her crown and greeted the elf. Sunny asked to borrow a pot of honey for his project.

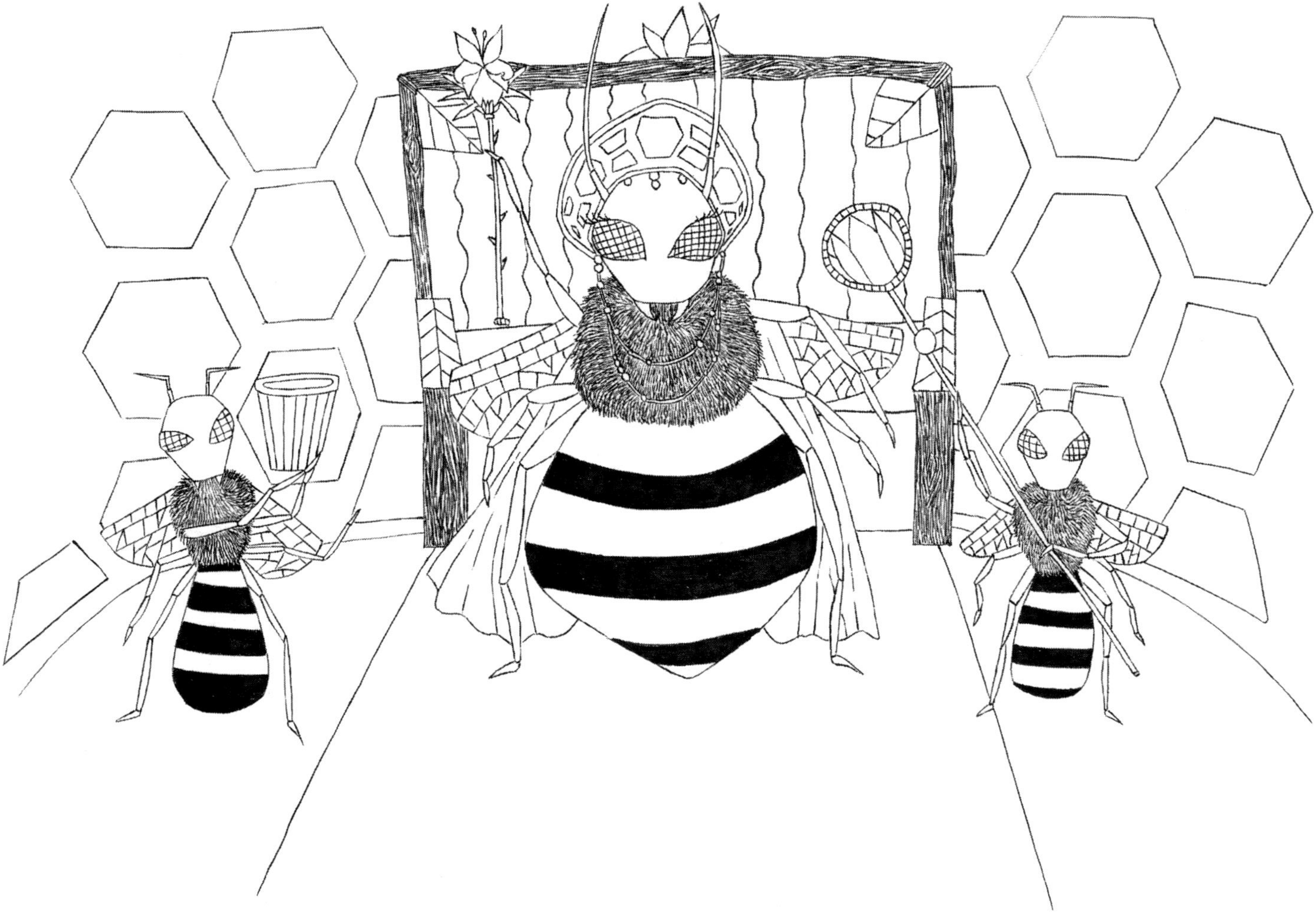

She would give him a pot if he helped her bees collect some honey. They were short on workers as many were sick that day. So off Sunny went! He giggled as he marched to the petunia fields and even buzzed along to their work song. Buzz. Buzz.

He carried pots back to the hive and into neat storage rooms. Once he was done with his task, the Queen Bee gave him a pot of honey and some bees wax as a reward for his help.

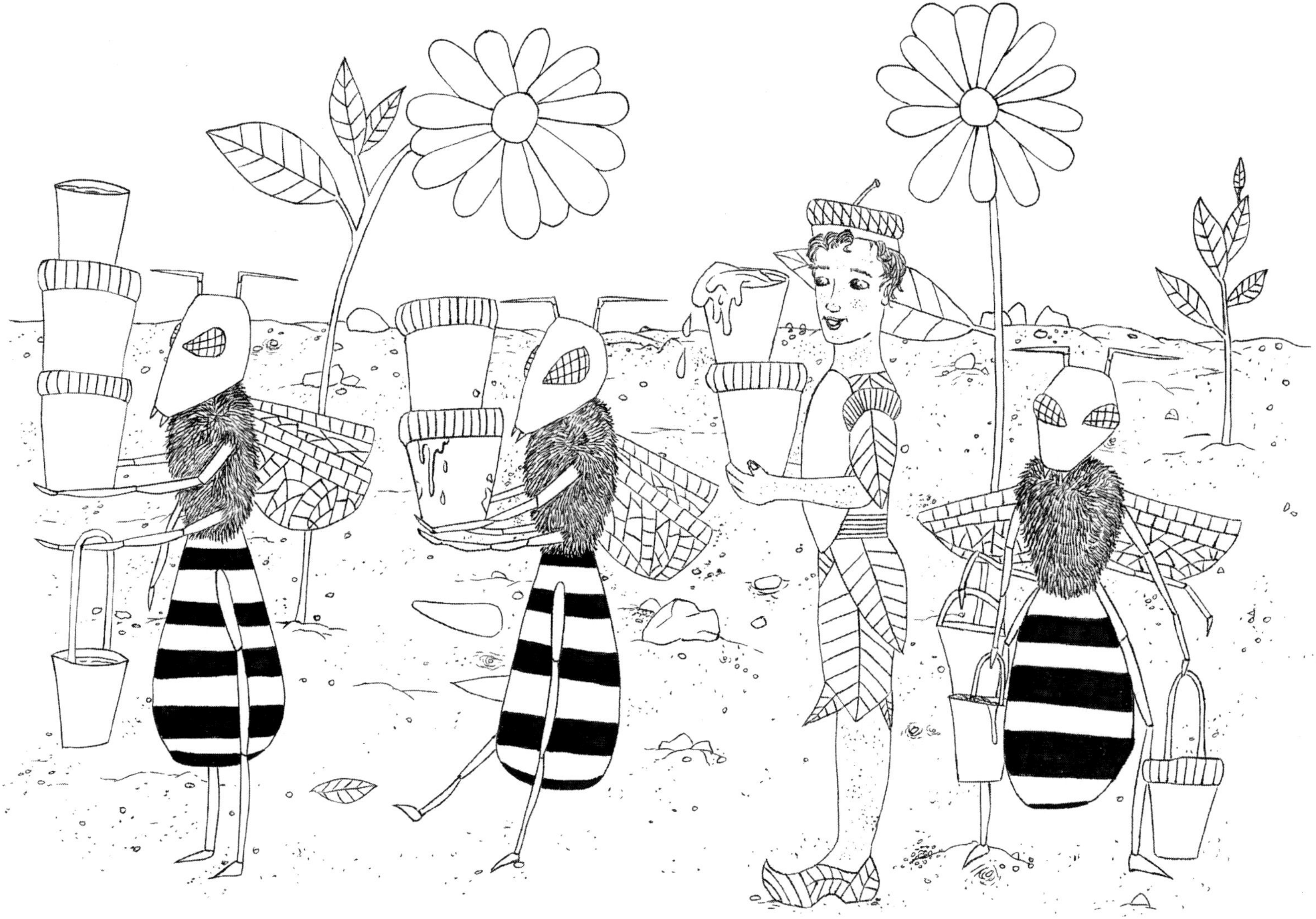

Sunny skipped home to finish his wings. He stuck his fingers into the thick honey and glued the sides together. Then he added a coat of beeswax. Now he just needed to wait for them to dry. He wondered what it would feel like to fly. He could already picture how much fun his friends were having while giggling up in the treetops.

When it dried, Sunny was sure it would work this time.

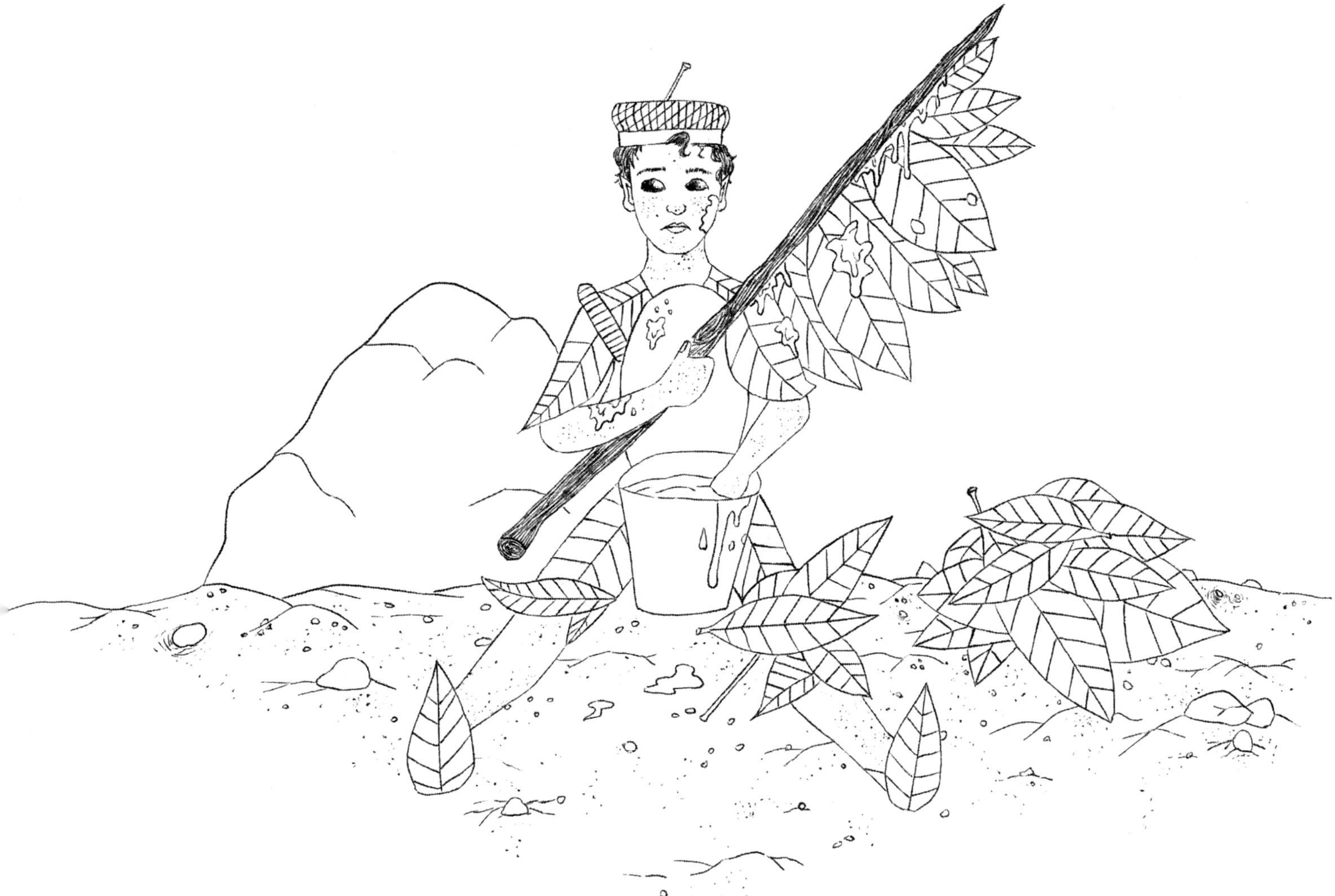

Sunny adjusted his flying goggles, straightened his wings and looked ahead. Running off the cliff, he flapped his wings as hard as he could. Harder and harder! HE WAS FLYING!

Sunny was flying like the fairies!

Soaring clumsily through the air, Sunny looked down. He didn't like it one bit. Sunny realized that he didn't like heights and flying was a big, big mistake. Flying was not what he expected. Before he knew it, the little elf crashed into the top branches of a tree. If he paid more attention to where he was going, he wouldn't have landed himself in such a sticky mess. Now he had no clue how to climb down.

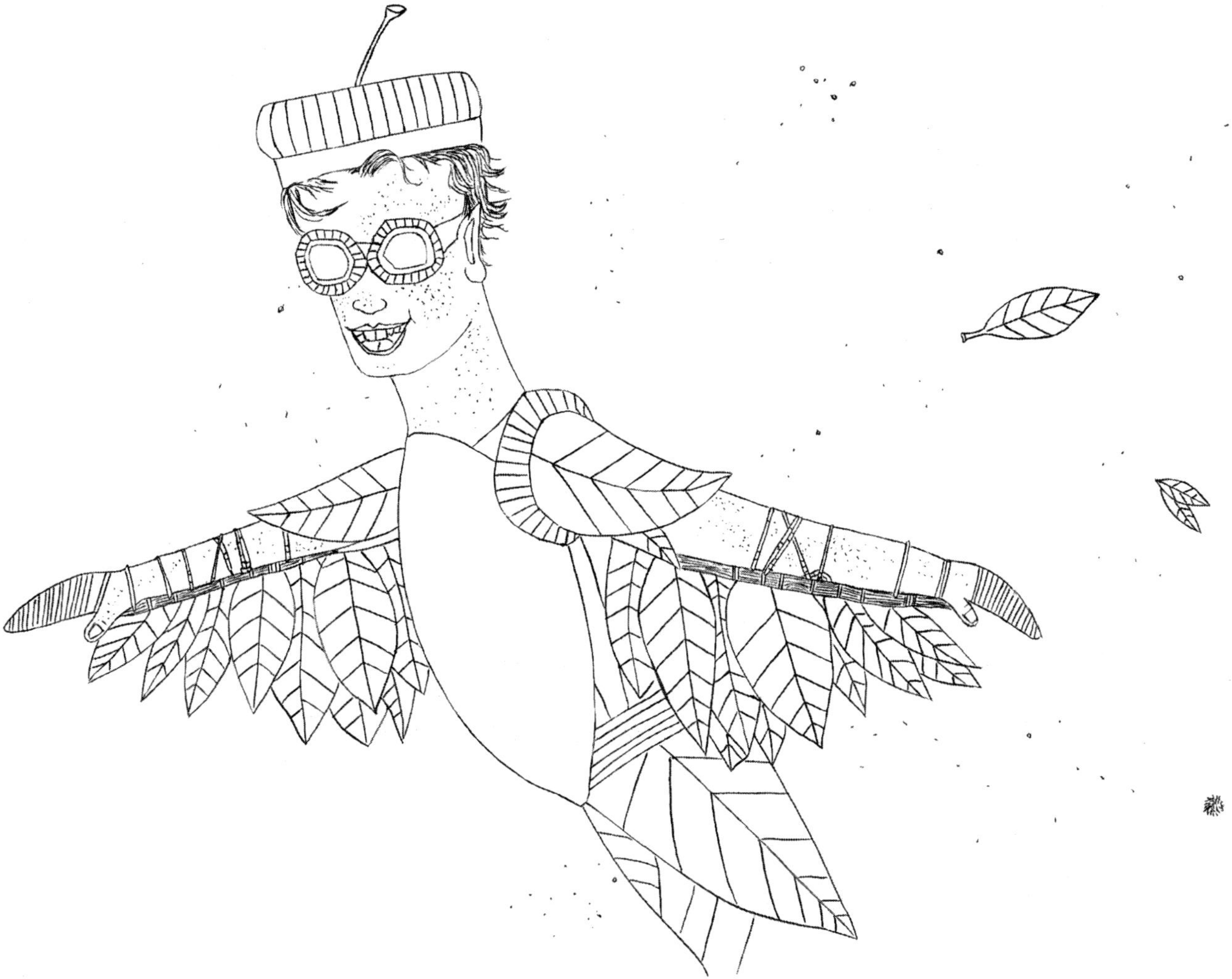

With the help of a squirrel looking for nuts in the tree, Sunny got the ride he needed. When he was on the ground, he turned to Lily calling out to him. She had dropped her hat into a hole but couldn't get it back herself. Small spaces would break a fairy's wings. This was a job for an elf!

Small, little Sunny could easily squeeze through
the hole and get Lily's bluebell hat.

"Thank you Sunny! You are always so helpful! You are a great friend. How I wish I can be like you and don't have to bother with these wings." said Lily as she gave him a hug.

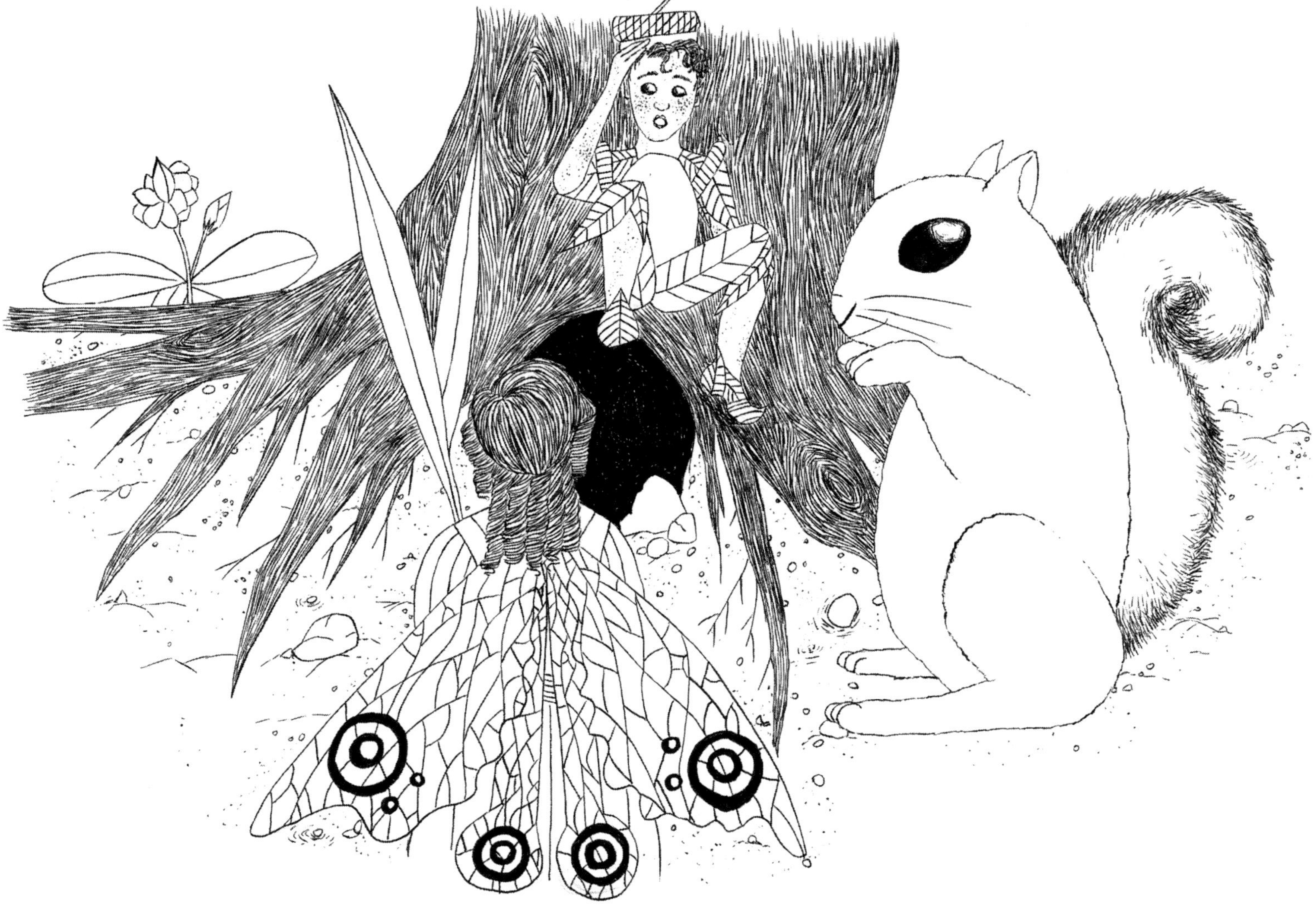

He stood and thought of his adventures that day. The clever little elf learned quite an important lesson. He didn't need wings to be a hero. Flying may be something he couldn't do but there were other things he was better at than his friends. His mother was right. He should always be happy with himself and who he was. Everyone has different talents. In this world, there will always be people with nicer things or people who could do things you can't do, but it is important to love and just be happy with yourself.

Big wings, little wings or no wings. Believing in yourself, is the greatest magic of all.

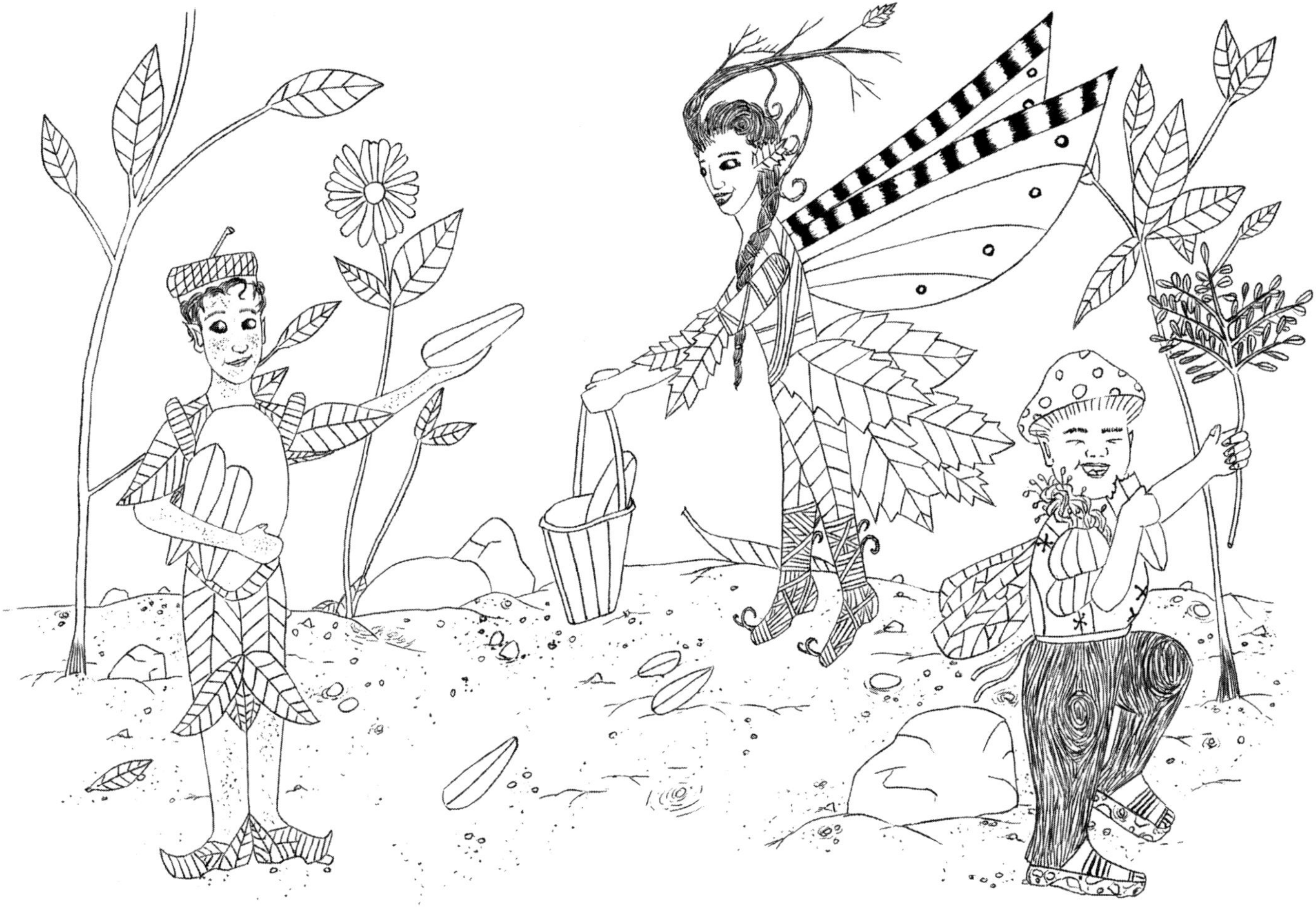